Naughty Indulgences: The Ultimate Birthday Gift

Safe Haven, Volume 2

Stephanie Doering

Published by Stephanie Doering, 2024.

This is a work of fiction. Similarities to real people, places, or events are entirely coincidental.

NAUGHTY INDULGENCES:THE ULTIMATE BIRTHDAY GIFT

First edition. December 9, 2024.

Copyright © 2024 Stephanie Doering.

ISBN: 979-8230549185

Written by Stephanie Doering.

Table of Contents

Chapter 1

Nine months ago, I came to Safe Haven with no idea what to expect, but now I knew what would be in store for me. Rhys, my boyfriend had taken me here to celebrate his birthday

and I agreed to come along clueless at first about what Safe Haven was about, but by the end of our weekend, my eyes had been opened to a whole new world. I left that weekend more assured of myself as a person, as a woman, and definitely when it came to sex. Today, Rhys and I along with our third, Braxton were returning to celebrate Braxton and my birthdays which are a day apart.

Maybe I should back up for a minute and tell you about Safe Haven because it is nothing like you have encountered before. Safe Haven is a sex club where people can come to live out some of their most erotic fantasies while maintaining the safety that Safe Haven provides for them in the world of BDSM. I should make myself clearer so that you understand. In the world of BDSM, you have bondage, sadists, masochists, sadomasochists, submissives, and dominants among other things at your disposal. When you are in the world of BDSM sometimes people's fetishes and kinks can cross the line into a more dangerous area like choking or asphyxiation. If you are not careful somebody could get seriously hurt or even die, which is where the master/submissive communication becomes critical.

What do I mean? Before you even attempt to play a scene at Safe Haven understand there is always a master and a submissive, but don't be fooled into thinking that just because you might be submissive you don't have a voice, because in reality, you do. Quite honestly, the submissive can set the tone of a scene allowing for it to go however far they wish it to go ahead of time. Both the master and submissive talk about it, and have a safe word to use in case there is a need to end the scene. On the off chance that you are into ball gags which renders you unable to speak, then you usually use a hand signal or some sort of object to signal that you wish the scene to end immediately.

BDSM is a lifestyle but not one that is for everyone. BDSM is very much a taboo subject since people associate it with being bad, but in reality, it doesn't have to be. Be that as it may, there is very much still a lot of secrecy that surrounds BDSM because of the judgments people place on you. When I first came to Safe Haven, I had no idea what would happen, but I trusted my boyfriend so that was a huge benefit from the get-go.

Rhys hadn't been the most forthcoming with me when we started dating to let me know that he was into BDSM. Truth be told Rhys never said anything to me until he asked me to go away for his birthday because he wanted to visit a club his friend owned. In his defense though, I had gotten out of an abusive relationship with a self-depreciating prick so I could understand Rhys' hesitancy to say anything when it came to anything relating to sex, and BDSM holding the bad connotations would have sent me running away from him.

When Rhys asked me to go to Safe Haven, immediately I jumped at the chance to go away with him and investigate a new club without knowing what it was all about. It was only after I agreed to go that he told me all about Safe Haven. Rhys had given me multiple opportunities to back out, but I chose to go because of the trust we had in our relationship. I was a little apprehensive at first, but now, I am glad that I went with him.

Rhys took a gamble when he proposed the idea of coming to Safe Haven, but it had been a calculated gamble. See, my ex-boyfriend Kincaid was an asshole who diminished the person I was especially when it came to sex. Long story short, Rhys and I lived in the same apartment complex but on different floors, and one night he was coming home from work and saw me arguing with Kincaid outside the building. When I told Kincaid we were through, he grabbed me roughly by the arm which was when Rhys stepped out from the shadows and broke Kincaid's nose. Eventually, the more time Rhys and I spent together the more we realized we wanted to be together as a couple, but he could always tell that there was a part of me that was unsure of herself when it came to sex.

You see, over time he slowly built the courage for me to trust him implicitly so that when he told me about Safe Haven, I didn't think twice about going because it was something he wanted to share with just me. As I said before, BDSM isn't for everyone, but this had been something Rhys wanted to share with me and I accepted. What I never expected was how it would make me feel. Rhys just had to get me passed my insecurities and realize it for myself. By the end of that weekend, I left Safe Haven more assured of the person I was, and Rhys and I were both ready to face our friends and tell them about our relationship that we'd kept secret from them for almost 8 months.

Now, this isn't to say that Rhys and I told them everything because we didn't. Rhys and I both had been friends since college and the group we ritualistically hang with have been friends of ours as well since freshman year in college, but they can be a bit judgmental. Honestly, your sex life should always remain just yours no matter how you enjoy it, whether it is straight missionary style or on St. Andrew's cross.

Like I was telling you, we told everybody about our relationship, and they were extremely happy for us, especially considering how horrible Kincaid had been. They had all hated him from the start. That friend group does not know about our interest in BDSM nor will they ever. Add in Braxton, the third in our relationship, yeah, that is something you don't normally talk about. How did Rhys and I end up with a third to our relationship, and what sort of relationship do we all have? I guess I should back up and tell you a bit more about what happened following my first visit to Safe Haven.

Rhys and I met Braxton at Safe Haven the weekend we went to play. Braxton was a master employed there by the owner and friend of Rhys, Bella, or in the BDSM world, Mistress Belladonna. Braxton and Rhys had played together all weekend, but I too had the chance to play with

Braxton and Rhys at one point, and I walked away feeling something else entirely different than I had at any other point that weekend. I don't know if I could put into words exactly how the encounter with Braxton felt except that I had changed and leaving Braxton, was going to be harder for me considering this was a man I just met.

When Rhys asked how I felt after playing with him and Braxton, I shockingly said I could see Braxton as our third, not just for playing, but in our relationship as a whole. Telling Rhys this surprised him because this was not something he would've ever expected from me. Ironically, Rhys informed me that Braxton had mentioned to him his interest in me and him, but he didn't want to step on Rhys' toes. Also, Rhys mentioned that Braxton was moving to our city for work since he was done with his doctorate in education with a specialty in counseling and had a job lined up. I jumped immediately at the opportunity that Braxton was affording us, and Rhys was more than happy to make it happen.

Yes, I know, I am glancing over a few key items, but I will return to them in a minute. Rhys and I called Braxton and told him how we both felt and when he moved here, he became our third.

Now, I can back up and tell you, that once Rhys and I got back from Safe Haven not only did we tell our friends about our relationship, but we also decided to take our relationship a step further and bought a small house. While it might seem like a huge step, both of us had been spending time at each other's apartments non-stop so paying rent on 2 apartments was stupid. Factor in Braxton was moving, and Rhys and I decided a house would be a good way for us to spend time with Braxton, where nobody would be the wiser.

When we approached Braxton about how Rhys and I were buying a house and we told him we wanted him to move in with us there was no hesitation, he was all in. By then he had already agreed to become our third and out of that we grew into our throuple. Rhys and I told him that as far as our friends were concerned, they were childhood friends with whom we were helping out and nobody would be the wiser of the lie we told.

Right from the start, Rhys, Braxton, and I set out what we wanted from the relationship, how we could date each other separately but also as a thruple. There was a lot of communication that was involved and there still is, but it seems to work for us.

Braxton had been moving his stuff to our house over a couple of weekends to allow him time to work still at Safe Haven before starting his new job here as a counselor. We had even gone ahead and given him his key so that he could come and go without us around.

Let me tell you about the weekend that Braxton was officially moving into the house. He had told Rhys and me that he'd be there Saturday, so after work that Friday night Rhys and I met the gang for wings and beer at Creepers our Friday night ritual. We were all sitting around our table talking, Rhys next to me like always, when Braxton slowly crept up behind us and covered my eyes with his hands and said, "Hey there beautiful," and then uncovered my eyes. As soon as I heard the words "Hey there beautiful," I didn't need to turn around to know who it was because I knew based on that sexy baritone voice it was Braxton. My heart skipped a beat, and I wore a smile like a lovesick puppy.

Rhys and I both jumped up from our chairs to greet Braxton. Rhys gave him the bro hug; you know the one where they hug and pat each other on the back. I wrapped my arms around Braxton hugging him and kissed him on his cheek as I joyfully squealed, "Braxton!" At that point, Rhys and I moved our seats apart to allow Braxton to sit in between us. Introductions were made, more beer and wings were ordered and thus began our ritualistic Friday nights that now included Braxton.

Chapter 2

Braxton, Rhys, and I spent the first week or so as a threesome cuddling, kissing, and talking about how to go about this relationship. We all agreed we wanted to date each other, both as a couple and as a threesome, but how did we split the time? This was an area none of us were familiar with but decided that we would just have to continue to communicate our needs effectively.

Dating both guys means there is a lot of give and take for all of us but especially for Braxton and Rhys since it is their nature to be dominating. Just like any other relationship, there is a lot of give and take to make things work. Oh, this doesn't mean that you still won't encounter bumps along the way, because you will, it is just a matter of how well you manage to handle them that can either allow the relationship to flourish or die.

There was a time when I would have scoffed at the idea of BDSM, but now I don't see how I couldn't have it in my life. Keeping that same forethought in mind there would have been a time when I scoffed at the idea of dating 2 men at once, but now, I am glad I am. I am truly deeply, madly in love with both men and I don't know if I could ever choose between one of them if I had to.

Yes, Rhys and I have been together longer, but Braxton, well, Braxton has earned the right to my heart and love. The relationship with both men especially when I am with them both doesn't feel complicated like it did with Kincaid. Yes, we all put in the time and effort to make it work, but then again you *have* to do that for any relationship to work, right? I really can't explain it because how do you put into words something so meaningful and something so deeply personal? You just can't but I will attempt to try.

I guess you can say my feelings for Rhys developed slowly over time because we had been friends. More importantly, I was scared of how I felt for him after my disastrous relationship with Kincaid. The moment I met Braxton at Safe Haven something inside me stirred to life. The same feelings I have for Rhys suddenly awoke with Braxton, only I had gotten them instantaneously. I never believed in love at first sight, but Braxton changed all that and that is not to diminish my relationship with Rhys. So that is why when I left Safe Haven that first weekend, I knew that I wanted him as a more permanent fixture in my life and not someone who was just around to do BDSM with besides Rhys.

Navigating the whole relationship together was tenuous at best when we first started, but that was because none of us had ever tried to have a threesome in terms of dating. Yes, the guys had threesomes when it came to sex, but that had been it – it was just sex. Since being in a relationship is more than just about sex, we have had to learn together how to navigate a relationship that involves multiple people. Learning together has been wonderful.

Whenever it came to sex with them both it was fantastic, but even on the nights when it was just Rhys and Braxton it was exceptional. Oh, the nights that Braxton and Rhys invited me to watch them but not be a part of the action between them created something else entirely. Watching those two together was steamy. Just being able to sit in a chair in the bedroom while the two most important men in my life are satisfying each other's sexual needs is self-gratifying. To sit and watch your two lovers enjoying each other whether it was watching them sucking on their cocks or fucking in their asses can be erotic and for me it was.

I will admit that hiding this relationship has become more difficult as time has gone on for us because the intensity of love that we share has only deepened. The first night Braxton showed up unexpectedly at Creeper's and I jumped up and wrapped my arms around him and kissed him on the cheek, I almost kissed him on the mouth passionately. Just looking at him made me want him and that slip-up could have meant the difference for the three of us when it came to the gang. We all know there will come a day when the three of us no longer are willing to hide our relationship and will want to tell everyone, and hopefully, when we do, they will accept it for what it is. Until then we find ways to be what we are which is why we decided to go back to Safe Haven for our birthdays.

To go out of town for our birthdays, we told our friends a half-truth. We were honest and said that we were going out of town for our birthdays, the lie, was that we were going back to Rhys and Braxton's hometown. Our friends bought the lie hook line and sinker and said that we'd have to celebrate the following Friday instead. Not only did we leave that Friday, but we also just took the day off and left when we wanted to. We are not ashamed of what we are, we just choose to not be judged because of it.

Nico, Gray, Damien, Lily, Jade, Samara, Rhys and I formed a bond our first semester at college our freshman year in English Lit. The fact that the eight of us have become this inseparable even after college is amazing, but this does not mean that Rhys and I are entirely confident that they would be willing to accept our lifestyle because that is not something you readily discuss. Besides we don't feel like they need to know either.

Setting some important ground rules for our relationship has made all the difference with the most important being communication. Many relationships struggle with communication when it is just two of you, but now because there's a third member to the relationship communication is that much more vital. I believe communication is probably the best thing we have going because we are not afraid to communicate our needs and our dislikes. Plus, we are willing to accommodate each other's needs. Recently, we had our first chance to put the lines of communication to work.

It was a night not too long ago when Rhys and Braxton were supposed to have a night for themselves, but I had come home late annoyed as all fuck. It had been a series of things that day compounding on top of one another until it felt as if the rug got pulled out from under me. I didn't get home until almost 9 p.m. well past my normal time, and Rhys and Braxton were in the bedroom that Rhys and I normally shared.

Now, I realize that I told you Braxton had been living with us, but I need to clarify a few things before I get back to my story. Our house had 2 good-sized bedrooms and a smaller one, which we used to store our BDSM paraphernalia. Rhys and I shared a king-sized bed, so we deemed that room the room where all three of us would sleep when we slept as a threesome. Further, it was the room that Rhys and I used, and Rhys and Braxton used when we took our turns. Additionally, Braxton and I would use his room when it was our turn, and the nights Braxton spent with Rhys I would spend in his bed. No, this was not a complicated setup but one I felt needed to be made for this recollection I am telling now.

The night in question I got home late from work irritated beyond anything you could have imagined. I hardly lose my cool, so the fact that I came home, and slammed the door shut while I mumbled a few choice curse words about my boss should lend itself credence as to how bad a day it was. I was the type of person who normally left her work issues at work and chose not to bring them home with her, but this particular night was the rule breaker. By this juncture, I hadn't had any food since my lunch break, half of which I had worked through to finish a project that was due. I was fine missing part of my lunch hour because I knew I could grab something to go on the way home or cook something quickly when I got home. I just never expected to end up staying until well after 8 p.m. to wrap up this super important project with my boss and not stop for dinner.

Now, it does not even dawn on me that this night was Rhys and Braxton's date night. I just automatically go to Rhys' and mine bedroom to get changed, but all I can see Rhys and Braxton naked in the throes of giving each other blowjobs. Seeing them there like that should have turned me on, but instead, it made me angry because at that moment I wanted to be the center of their world. I needed them. I just look at them with the other's cock in their mouth and shout, "Fuck!" and throw my heels into the room all while storming out of the bedroom, hurrying as fast as I could to the kitchen. Both guys scrambled off the bed as rapidly as they could run after me all while yelling, "Mack, Mack! Wait for us, please!"

Braxton got to me first. He grabbed me by the arm pulled me to his naked body and just held me saying nothing. Rhys came up behind me embracing me as well, so that his naked body was against my ass, and his hands caressed Braxton's back. We just stayed like that for a minute before I apologized to them profusely, "Oh guys, I am *so* sorry. I forgot you guys had a date tonight." Tears started to fall down my face, tears that were once for anger turned to sadness that I had interrupted and possibly ruined their night.

"Hey, hey, shh!" Rhys said trying to calm me down. "Why don't we all go back into the bedroom and sit for a minute, and you can tell us what's wrong? Ok?"

Rhys, the voice of reason at that moment all I could do was nod in agreement and let Braxton and Rhys lead me to the bedroom. There in the bedroom, they both took pleasure in undressing me until I was naked and then had me sit between them so they could both offer me comfort. They didn't have anything planned for us, they just wanted to make sure I was out of my work clothes, which would in turn relax me a bit.

I sighed, my head resting on Braxton's shoulder as he kissed the top of my head, while Rhys stroked my thigh. I just all of a sudden let it all out. "It's just been a series of unfortunate events today at work. I haven't eaten since lunch and hell; I worked through half of my lunch break. I didn't leave the office until sometime after 8 and I just wanted to crawl into bed and curl up under the covers and forget about today."

"Well," Rhys said, "Braxton and I can help you a little bit. Why don't you stay here with Braxton while I heat you some of our leftovers from dinner tonight? I made Chicken Cacciatore. Once, you have eaten that can solve part of this issue."

"Ok." I agreed with Rhys and said nothing else as I tried to catch my breath between sobs.

Alone with Braxton, I just kept mumbling about how sorry I was for ruining their night. Braxton lifted my head so he could look me in the eyes and said, "Mackenzie darling, you didn't ruin anything. You have a need that supersedes anything that Rhys and I might've been doing. You are an integral part of this relationship, and right now you are broken, let us both help you."

I couldn't look at Braxton and be upset, sad, angry, or anything because of what he had said to me. He was right, I needed both him and Rhys to help me and take care of me at that moment. Instinctively I curled up into his lap his arms embracing me, comforting me until Rhys came back with a steaming plate of chicken cacciatore.

Having satisfied the food aspect of my hunger, I needed to satisfy the rest of it. I needed to tell them what I wanted, and I wanted them both. I took a hand of each of my men and asked them, "Can you both lay with me and hold me? I need to feel both of you right now."

"Of course," Rhys said as he kissed me on the lips reassuring me of his commitment to us.

As I lay with them, I felt safe and warm. I felt whole again. I had expected something more to happen between us, but instead, I fell asleep until morning with both of them holding me all night long. It was nice, and definitely what I had needed at that moment. Looking back now, I definitely can see how important the lines of communication to my lovers were at that moment because I had been broken and what I needed was comfort, the comfort that only they could provide for me. It was a comfort that would not have happened had I not told them what I needed.

Chapter 3

In nine months since the three of us became a thruple, Braxton has gone to Safe Haven by himself or even with Rhys, and the same for me, but we have never gone as a threesome.

Now, here we are driving a couple hours from home to spend the weekend at Safe Haven. We were staying at the same hotel Rhys, and I stayed at nine months ago since it was extremely close to Safe Haven.

Since today was Braxton's birthday, Rhys and I wanted to celebrate with him first by treating him to dinner at his choice of restaurants before we headed over to Safe Haven to play. Plus, we had a very special birthday present for him that we wanted to give him in the hotel room after dinner. I couldn't wait for Braxton to get his birthday present. Rhys and I decided to get Braxton a new outfit for playing. We got him a black leather zip-up vest with a black leather jockstrap, and a leather crop and we couldn't wait to see him in it later, but first dinner.

After checking into the hotel, we put our luggage in our room and asked Braxton to choose where he'd like to go for dinner tonight for his birthday. Braxton said that there was a seafood restaurant down the block that had killer crab legs and lobster, and he could already taste it in his mouth. He didn't need to tell us anymore because it was his birthday after all, and this was part of his special day.

Braxton had not lied when he said that the restaurant had killer crab legs and lobster. They had some of the freshest Alaskan king crabs I had ever had, and how I had been able to eat as much food as I did was surprising. Then again, we were going to work it off once we got to Safe Haven that was just a given.

Back at the hotel following dinner, Rhys and I gave Braxton his birthday present. He unwrapped the present and loved the new outfit he had gotten and decided he would wear it tonight. He said he was saving the crop for another time because he wanted to try it out on both

Rhys and me. He thanked Rhys first with a kiss on the mouth with a very hot French kiss. When they were done kissing, Braxton pulled me to him and held me, as he leaned down and pressed his mouth to mine and kissed me, my arms wrapping around his neck. Honestly, if we didn't have places to be, I swear I would have taken this man and had my way with him.

Arriving at Safe Haven after being away for 2 months felt invigorating. I couldn't wait to explore more of myself and my likes and dislikes. We immediately went to the changing rooms and changed out of our street clothes and into our play clothes. I had expanded my wardrobe since that weekend 92 months ago. Tonight, I opted for a red zip-up skintight micro mini-dress that barely covered my ass, no bra or panties, thigh-high red leather boots, and a black lace seduction hood. When I stepped out of the dressing room Braxton immediately said, "Fuck me, she's on fire tonight, she's so hot." Rhys could only stare at me and utter a "mm hm" back at Braxton. I smiled because I knew that I was off to a good start now, especially with my lover's erect just from seeing my outfit.

Just then Mistress Bella sashayed her way over to us looking stunning as she always did. "Happy birthday, Braxton darling!" She exclaimed as she kissed him before kissing Rhys. Turning to me she said, "Mackenzie, darling stunningly beautiful. I so enjoy that outfit. You *must* go play with Eros. I believe he would be the perfect one for you tonight." I couldn't help but smile at Bella and say to her, "Thank you, Mistress. Will you be joining us, or will it just be Master Eros and I?" Bella started to laugh, "Unfortunately, it will just be you two. Tonight, I have Rhys since I still have yet to punish him for that faux pas the first time you both were here," I couldn't help it, I laughed as Rhys gulped but went ahead with the plans Bella had put together. "And for Braxton," she began as she smiled at him, "Mistress Cassidy is in the chamber waiting for you. She is setting up for your birthday session with her. I truly think she has missed playing with you because she has pulled out all the stops."

Braxton blushed, something he doesn't do often, and said, "As do I, but I quite enjoy the company that these two give me. Although, I wouldn't mind if you happened to stop by our session tonight to remind me about how talented you are as a mistress."

Bella beamed proudly at Braxton's response and then said, "We did hire a new master finally since one of everyone's favorites went on to better things. Hmm, maybe you should have him tonight Braxton this way you can tell me exactly what you think of him." Pausing for a moment to contemplate her response Bella went on to say, "Yes, yes that is what I will do! I will send him to the chamber to meet you and Cassidy. Perfect!" Bella clapped her hands excitedly and had him scurry off to the dungeon while I found Eros in his room.

Stepping into Eros' room is like stepping back to the medieval times with tons of torture devices. Eros is a sadomasochist and most people who come to play cannot take his level of torture – erm I mean fun. While most people are either submissive or dominant, some are called switches because they can easily be both submissive and dominant and I happen to be a switch.

Bella doesn't do anything without a reason when it comes to play at Safe Haven. She knows her staff and their most dominant traits, kinks, and fetishes. Now the people that come to play at Safe Haven, she likes to learn a little about them first so that she can make sure that they are put in the right room with the right master. Tonight, I was entering Eros' lair, and while many would question whether or not putting me with Eros was the right decision, I knew that Bella wanted to test my measure more and Eros was the right one to do it for her. Eros was not only Bella's significant other, but he was her right-hand man here at Safe Haven so he would report back to her concerning our time together.

"Good evening, Master Eros," I said politely to him as I entered his domain. I was now inside the world of master versus submissive and not acknowledging the status of a master could end up with some sort of punishment. Although some punishments are fun to take, I wasn't a fool where Eros was concerned. I knew that he was a stickler when it came to proper protocol although I have seen him slip a time or two with Bella.

"Mackenzie! You look radiant tonight. I will go ahead and say it now, you look sexy and extremely confident, much more so than you were nine ago when you first came. Hell, you are spicier than you were even two months ago when you were here."

I blushed at the compliment from Eros because it was a compliment that he did not have to offer but did, which meant a lot to me. "Thank you, Master Eros. I am looking forward to tonight with you."

Eros looked at me with an eyebrow raised. "Really? There will be nobody here tonight, just us and I am the Master in this domain."

I took a step forward toward Eros looked him in the eyes and said in the most confident tone I could find, "I am very aware that this is your domain. Do not hold back because it is me, Master Eros. Same words as last time, red, yellow, and green?"

Eros stepped forward grabbed an arm and pulled me to him and crushed his mouth to mine. I heartily accepted his mouth and gladly met it with lips parted, tongue darting out to explore his mouth and then he broke our kiss just as quickly as he instigated it. A sadistic smile crossed his lips and he said, "I am *so* going to enjoy tonight with you my dear. Just so we are clear, repeat for me what red, yellow, and green stand for in this room."

"Yes, Master Eros. Red means stop, I hate it. Yellow is a warning that we are not fully loving it but not yet hating it and that we need to stop. Green means that I am extremely satisfied with what you are doing, and you may continue."

"Excellent my dear. Excellent. Climb onto the submission horse on your hands and knees so that I may strap your wrists and ankles."

Obediently I climbed onto the horse got on my hands and knees looked at Eros and asked, "Like this Master?"

"Perfect Mackenzie. Again, please do not hesitate to tell me if I need to adjust something to make you a bit more comfortable. Okay?"

"Very well Master Eros." I was quite excited to be with Eros tonight because I knew he would push me much more than the other masters or mistresses would. I might be newer to the world of BDSM, but I am not going to break because of a little pain.

Eros immediately started by placing a black nylon hood over my head so that everything was covered except for my nostrils and mouth. I wouldn't be able to see anything and would be relying on my other senses. I wish I could say that this wasn't turning me on, but it was. I was enjoying it very much so and Eros could tell.

"Mackenzie, for now, you are not allowed to come and if you do, you will be punished severely. Do you understand?"

"Yes, Master Eros, no coming until you tell me to do so or suffer the consequences for insubordination."

I heard Eros mumble "fuck she's hot" before regaining his composure and saying, "Perfect." Secretly I was smiling at knowing I was getting to Eros. When I could get the sadomasochist to lose his composure then I knew I was in my element.

I could feel Eros's hands on my ass, but I was not sure what he was going to do. All I know is that he pushed the hem of my dress up to my waist to allow for better access to do what he wished for me. He rubbed a hand on my ass before he spanked me hard as he could on my bare ass, and he continued to do so as I moaned in sheer pleasure from the spanks but silently reminded myself, I could not come per his instructions.

Just when I thought I was going to come he switched from spanking me to flogging me. "Ouch!" I shouted at first as I felt the cold chain metal wallop my behind as I slowly grew accustomed to the flogging. "Green!" I shouted as he continued to flog me a little harder each time. "Oh Fuck!" I screamed. I didn't realize just how enjoyable this flogging with chain metal was for me.

"You are enjoying this pain aren't you, Mackenzie?" Eros asked me.

Through breaths, I answered, "Y-yes Master I am. It's so hard for me to not come from the pleasure it is causing me."

I heard that sadistic chuckle of Eros' as he reminded me, "Very good, but you still cannot come yet. Now, I am going to switch it up just a bit."

I obliged and said, "Yes Master."

The next time Eros swatted my ass it felt as if I had been electrocuted. "Oh fuck, what is that?" I asked slipping out of character.

Eros maniacally laughed. "I should punish you for not asking me properly, but I needed to know how this thing worked. It's a brand-new electroshock paddle. You are the very first to test it and receive the shocks."

"I'm sorry Master for not asking properly that shock caught me off guard, that is all."

"Mackenzie, that is fine. But how do you feel about it?"

"Permission to speak freely for a moment?" I asked Eros because I wanted to drop the Master for a moment.

"Permission granted," he said.

I spoke from the heart. "Seriously Eros, I am quite unsure if I like it or not. Imagine your cock being electrocuted without warning. How would you feel? I think for now you need to continue."

Eros started to laugh. "You paint such an exquisite picture, Mackenzie. I understand tonight why Bella said you were a switch. I am extremely pleased with how far you have come these past nine months. I believe Rhys and Braxton have been good for you."

"T-thank you, master but you are as much to thank as Rhys and Braxton are," I said as Eros continued the electroshock paddling for a bit before switching back to the chain metal flogger which immediately warranted me hollering, "Yellow!" as he continued to flog me until I finally yelled, "Red!" and he stopped the flogging.

Immediately following the flogging, Eros took a Wartenberg Pinwheel and glided it over my bare ass. Backing up for a moment, I should explain what a Wartenberg Pinwheel is. It is a stainless-steel wheel with spikes that glide over the skin which used to be used primarily by doctors for neurological testing but has been used in BDSM for heightened sensation. My ass was already sore from the flogging and electroshock paddling he had done, so when the ice-cold metal Wartenberg wheel was lightly raked over my ass I immediately bellowed, "Green. Oh fuck, green!" The pleasure was coursing throughout me, and I wasn't sure if I could hold back from orgasm.

Eros immediately stopped utilization of the Wartenberg Pinwheel removed the hood from my head and unstrapped me from the submission horse. I was left pining for release, none of which I had yet, but had closed on many occasions.

Next, Eros got me naked and then put me into the stockade much to my chagrin. I was not a fan by any means of having my neck strapped into something while I am on my hands and knees spread eagle and cuffed as well. Eros knew this too since he was present the first time they tried the stockade on me. However, unlike last time, I did not immediately protest like a good submissive would and waited to see what he had in store for me.

The very first thing that Eros did was insert a butt plug which only heightened the sensations throughout my body. My body was being racked with pleasure and not allowed to do anything about it. It was pure torture, and I knew that this was getting Eros aroused. While I had the butt plug in, Eros, went ahead and placed nipple clamps on each of my nipples. Once they were in place, Eros immediately added the shock part to it all. "Ah fuck!" I screamed as pleasure coursed through me. I loved the feeling of the shock on my nipples- it felt so erogenous. If I could come I would, but I had been denied that pleasure and I was doing my best to try to not come.

Eros continued to dial up the shock until he had dialed it up to a level 7 and I called it "Red." The pleasure was starting to turn to pain, and I couldn't be sure if it was because of the need to have an orgasm and come extremely hard, or if it was because of my neck not being able to be moved. In any event, I called it and he stopped. Eros removed the nipple clamps from me and then released me from the stockade.

Offering me a hand, Eros gently said, "Come, Mackenzie, let us take a quick break on the chaise, and have a drink and a little food. I believe it will invigorate us a bit more."

"Thank you, Master Eros," I politely said to him.

"Mackenzie, please call me by my given name Dimitri while we relax. You have earned the pleasure to call me it, something I don't ever do or allow with submissives."

I looked at Eros stunned because he had just requested that I call him by his actual name. I couldn't help but smile. I couldn't help but ask him, "So why go by Eros when Dimitri is a perfectly suitable name?"

"Dimitri in Greek means earth-lover, but I feel like Eros the god of Love and Sex fits me better."

I couldn't help but laugh. "Ok, you got me there. It is quite fitting of you though." I said finishing the last of my drink and snack.

I followed Eros to a bed that he had in the room and waited for him to tell me what was next. Sensing I was waiting for my next command Eros said, "Undress me and then you can get on the bed and lay down on your back and wait for me."

Have you ever tried to peel a man out of a form-fitted black and red latex pants, with black boots? I can tell you that it is quite difficult, and I don't mean taking the boots off him either. Anyhow, once I had him naked, I seductively crawled onto the bed occasionally shaking my behind until I got to the pillows and laid down as Eros had instructed me.

Climbing into bed, Eros lay on his side facing me as he stroked my hair he leaned down and kissed me on the lips. My lips met his and parted to allow him entrance with his tongue into my mouth. The kiss wasn't rushed, but it was filled with passionate need. Not only had this man denied me all night of the ability to come, but he had denied himself the same pleasure as his 9" erection had indicated to me.

His erection was beautiful, and I needed to taste it. I had tasted him before, and I wanted to taste it again, but he was still in charge and I was the submissive, or was I? Right now, I didn't know.

Breaking his kiss, he said to me, "I need to taste that pussy of yours that has been denied release all night. And now I grant you release." I responded with a "And I need to have your cock inside my mouth. I need to taste you."

Not wanting to deny us pleasure, Eros gave me his cock to suck as he began to lick and suck my clit. "Oh god," I moaned with his cock inside my mouth as the wetness seeped from my pussy.

"Fuck Mackenzie, so wet for me," he said as he continued to lick and suck on my clit, adding a finger to it as well which immediately caused me to orgasm, my juices flowing from me as Eros greedily lapped at it.

Meanwhile, I continued to love his cock with my mouth fully around it until he hit the back of my throat. My tongue slowly glided over his rigid member flicking the head ever so gently and then pressing on the vein there. His cock danced in my mouth, and Eros moaned, "Oh God. Yes!" I could tell he was close because I could taste the precum dripping from his tip.

"Stop Mackenzie. I don't want to come in your mouth. I need to come inside your pussy." Eros begged of me, and I stopped, happy to welcome his cock into my pussy who was more than ready for him.

Eros quickly mounted me and thrust his erection deep into my pussy. When he rammed his rod into me, I gasped, "Oh yes!" in delight. "You feel so good," I said as he held himself there for a moment, he kissed my mouth as he started gyrating his hips against mine until a rhythm was had and our bodies met with urgent need and he slid his ramrod in, and out. I was already orgasming again, after having been denied for so long tonight, but now he was allowing me the pleasure I needed. "Harder Dimitri," I begged of him. I wanted him rough and hard the need was too great to have it any other way.

Obliging me, Eros threw my legs over his shoulders and began to pound my pussy harder, faster and deeper. The need to pound me was too great even for him to deny as both of us needed it. I could feel him growing harder inside of me, and I knew he was close. As he thrust himself deep inside of me my muscles constricted around his cock as I screamed from the orgasm washing over me, harder than I had ever come before. Unable to do much else, Eros erupted deep inside of me, coating me with his sticky semen. I could feel him shooting load after load until he had shot close to three huge loads inside of me.

Eros lay there holding me for a bit. "Mackenzie, I need to know if you are ok with everything that happened here tonight."

I looked at him and said, "Dimitri, I would have stopped you if I wasn't fine with it. I need you to know that."

"Thank you, Mackenzie. I appreciate it. Are your ass cheeks sore?" He asked smiling while a tint of red rose to his cheeks.

I giggled because I didn't think I had ever seen him blush before, but he was now. I looked at him and through my laughter tried to tell him why I was laughing, but couldn't control myself. So, Eros being who he is sat on top of me and started to tickle me causing me to squeal until I shouted, "Red!"

I shook my head at him and said, "You're so evil Dimitri," but he could tell that I was joking with him and kissed him again on the lips. "But seriously, I am laughing because I got to see you blush. I didn't think you got embarrassed."

Dimitri looked at me and muttered, "Ah fuck," and then went quiet. Concerned I sat up and looked at him in the eyes and requested he tell me what was bothering him. "Dimitri, talk to me. Something is bothering you. Was it something I did? What is going on?"

He sat there and sighed for a moment. "I care for Bella, I do. She's a fine partner in all things, but damn woman you are completely in your element when you are with me here in my domain. Add in I know you despise the stockade because you hate having your neck bound like you did, but you took it and didn't request for me to stop or anything." All while he rambled, I sat there staring at him, unsure what to say.

I placed a hand on him as I said to him, "You are Eros and Dimitri. They are the same. Don't be so hard on yourself because you enjoyed yourself immensely with someone other than Bella. I love Braxton and Rhys, yet tonight I enjoyed myself with you. Surprisingly, I feel like you can teach me more about the things I like than I think anyone could have imagined, me included."

"Mackenzie, in all the years I have been a Master a, I never have come inside a woman's pussy. Her mouth or her ass hole yes, pussy no. Tonight was a first."

"Dimitri, do you regret it?" I looked at him, a bundle of emotions running through him. It was odd to see him so unsure of himself.

"No, Mackenzie I don't," he said as he pulled me to him. "I wish I did, but I don't, and I would do it again in a heartbeat if I could with you."

Just then, there was a knock at his door and Bella entered the room. "Just letting you know we are all waiting for you both, but I can see that you are giving each other some aftercare. I will let them know," she said and walked out of the room.

"Dimitri, you are growing as a master. It's ok to cross the lines that you once had established. This whole world is not straight black and white, you of all people should know that. There are going to be moments when the lines get blurred, and you and I are just going to be the couple that when we are alone and playing, we might blur the lines occasionally. We just might need to communicate more during our scenes. We both want pleasure, and pain gives us both pleasure, but how we find our release is something I think we need to learn when playing."

"Get dressed Mackenzie before I have everyone barging into my domain," he said laughing at me. "Oh, I don't doubt that you will continue to teach me a few things my little switch just like you have tonight."

Hand in hand Eros and I walked out of the room laughing while everyone stood there with their mouths agape because we were the ones most unlikely to be laughing after a scene, but we were the ones who were. He was quickly becoming someone I enjoyed being with and around. I felt myself falling for him as something more than a friend, something that could shake the foundation of the triad I was in. Why wasn't I more concerned about that prospect? I don't know.

"Rhys, I will text you later with the details for tomorrow," Bella said to him as we all walked up front together to get changed.

Chapter 4

After leaving Safe Haven with Rhys and Braxton, we all stopped at a deli that stayed open late to pick up some subs to eat when we got back to the hotel room since we were famished from playing and needed to replenish the calories we had burnt off.

Once we were safely behind the door to our room, we all said hello the proper way with very long kisses. Rhys kissed me on the mouth while Braxton was kissing my neck. I was torn between food and loving these two handsome men with whom I had yet the pleasure to be with since before Safe Haven. Braxton made the decision quite easy since he took it upon himself and unzipped my dress allowing it to gather in a pool of golden cloth at my feet as I stood there naked while they were both fully clothed.

Braxton smiled at me as he said, "Mm, much better don't you think Rhys?"

Rhys smiled back at Braxton and said, "Oh it will be. I think we are a tad bit overdressed for the occasion. Don't you agree?" Rhys just casually moved toward Braxton ignoring the fact I was standing there and grabbed him by the shirt and pulled him to him and kissed him. While they kissed, they quickly undid the buttons on their shirts before parting from their kiss and finished undressing. In the meantime, I lay on the bed captivated by the scene unfolding before me. I always found it beautiful and sexy when they undressed each other.

Both Rhys and Braxton climbed onto the bed one on each side of me, Braxton kissing me while Rhys licked and sucked on my pussy. Kissing Braxton I could taste the hint of whiskey and knew that he had some while he was with Cassidy. I can't be jealous because it was his birthday, and he and Cassidy while both dominants used to play together quite often, so it was no surprise that she had his favorite liquor on hand. Braxton's hand caressed my breast and tweaked the nipple making it hard, as his tongue trailed down my neck until he found that breast and flicked the nipple with his tongue.

"Mm. Oh god, you both that feels so good," I moaned as I took Rhys's cock in my mouth and started to suck on it. I could feel him growing harder the more I licked and sucked him as my mouth surrounded his engorgement taking it fully. I continued with this motion, and occasionally my tongue would probe the hole at the tip of his cock causing it to jump in excitement. "Fuck Mack, I am so close!" Rhys exclaimed, his dick pulsing inside my mouth while Braxton licked my pussy and inserted his fingers in there as well. The feelings overwhelmed my senses, and I came hard from the pleasures both men were creating. I continued to suck Rhys' cock until he came inside my mouth.

Meanwhile, Braxton savored the moment as he buried his face in my pussy, his tongue flicked and kissed at my vulva. I could feel his warm breath down there and it aroused me even more. My body was in overdrive between Rhys and Braxton, and I was enjoying every minute, every sensation that coursed through me. Braxton continued to love my nether region by inserting two fingers into my clit as his tongue and mouth explored me more while he sucked at it. With his tongue flicking over my clitoris the sensations in me grew exponentially until I came, and Braxton lapped up my juices that flowed from me.

Switching positions, Rhys kissed me now and fondled my breasts while Braxton shoved his erection towards my mouth. My body arched from the orgasm that Rhys had already managed to create. All this teasing was making me want them even more, but I had to taste Braxton first. I needed to feel his hard member inside my mouth and so I licked the tip of his cock with my tongue and immediately swallowed his member down my throat as far as I could take it and began sucking on him taking him as deep as I could in my mouth. "Ah fuck Mack, you're going to make me come if you keep this up," Braxton said.

I continued to take Braxton's cock sucking it harder and faster as my mouth stayed secured around it not letting him go. At the same time Rhys was biting my nipple, I started to come while Braxton shot his load down my throat swallowing it all.

While I licked Braxton's cock clean, he was busy cleaning Rhys' cock and Rhys sucked on my nipple. Our moans echoed throughout the room, and I knew that both of my lovers were hard again and ready for more.

I climbed on top of Braxton and positioned my vagina so that it was angled to slide right onto his pole. As I sat down on his hard cock, we both stilled for a moment before we moved a little so that we were in the proper position so that Rhys could penetrate my ass with his erection. As Rhys's cock slowly spread my hole, he thrust it deeper until my hole had spread to allow him full entrance to the back and then he started to thrust his cock in my asshole while Rhys' pelvis gyrated against mine. His cock was pounding my pussy hard with each thrust. I could feel both of them inside me moving in rhythm as both entrances got fucked.

I kissed Braxton on the mouth and his lips parted allowing for my tongue to explore him while he continued to thrust his cock deeper inside my pussy. "Fuck!" I screamed as it felt as if his cock was touching Rhys', but I knew that it wasn't. They both were pounding me a little harder and faster with each thrust and I knew they were both close when I felt that familiar sensation of an orgasm hitting me hard. "Mm, oh yeah" I moaned as I came my body shuddering in delight and my muscles constricting around Braxton's cock milking it while Rhys' cock erupted inside my ass until I had both ends dripping from their come.

Cuddled together, we lay there and immediately fell asleep. When I woke a couple of hours later sandwiched between my lovers, I could feel both of them sporting a hard-on and smiled. I knew immediately how to rectify the situation as I ground my ass into Rhys' semi-erect cock as I kissed Braxton on the lips while my hands stroked his erection. Both men woke up immediately just as I had planned. Rhys grabbed my hips and ground his cock against my ass as it grew harder while he kissed the nape of my neck. Meanwhile, as I stroked Braxton's cock, precum dripped from its head and he met my mouth with his. "Fuck Mack!" he exclaimed as I continued to stroke his cock, feeling it grow in my grasp. Quickly I mounted Braxton allowing his cock to penetrate my vagina and sit there a moment while Rhys took me from behind and penetrated my vagina.

"Oh fuck!" I exclaimed as I felt both men's erect penises inside my pussy stretching me and starting to thrust in and out of me. Braxton sucked on my nipple while pounding me, and Rhys grabbed my hair in his fist and pulled on it as he hammered his cock in and out of me. My body shuddered with delight as the men continued to pump their cocks deep inside my pussy as she continued to seep her juices. Nothing but our moans and slap of skin on the skin could be heard in the room. Beads of perspiration glistened on our skin from the workout we were getting.

I couldn't help it, nothing else compared to when your lovers are both balls deep inside you and bringing nothing but sheer ecstasy to what had already been a fantastic night. "Oh God! Oh God!" I moaned as another orgasm racked my body and my vaginal muscles tightened like a vice and both Rhys and Braxton bellowed, they were coming as hot semen shot from them both coating the inside of my walls until they were both spent.

Rhys collapsed on the bed, and I rolled off of Braxton and lay next to them both as we were all once again satiated from our sexual encounter. Sleep claimed us all quickly and we slept peacefully for the remainder of the night.

The next time we woke the sun was streaming into our hotel room and my stomach was growling in hunger. Yawning I asked the guys, "What time is it?"

Looking at his phone, Rhys said, "9:23 a.m."

"Damn, I am starving," I said as I sat up. "I just realized we skipped eating the subs we bought on the way home instead of opting for sex and sleep," I giggled.

"Well, why don't we all eat our subs now, shower and dress, and then maybe start the birthday celebrations for you Mack? What do you think Braxton?" Rhys asked as he got up and went over to the refrigerator to get our subs.

Braxton looking handsome as ever smiled and said, "Oh I think we could start the birthday celebrations now," as he rolled over on top of me kissing me on the mouth as we exchanged saliva. In the background, I could hear Rhys stifling a laugh as he unwrapped his sub and took a quick bite of it while he let Braxton have his way with me.

My hands wrapped around the nape of Braxton's neck as I leaned up to meet his kisses with eagerness while he spread my legs apart with a knee and positioned himself so that his cock was touching the entrance to my clit but not yet inside of it. Leaning up to him, I gently bit Braxton's neck and heard him murmur "fuck" as he drove his cock hard into my pussy causing me to gasp in delight.

Thrusting his pelvis down, Braxton's cock rammed deep into me his balls slapping against my bare skin. "Oh fuck!" I exclaimed as Braxton rammed his cock in and out of me all while he kissed me on my mouth as our tongues explored the other's mouth. "Harder," I begged as I wrapped my legs around his waist my pussy already wet with need.

Grabbing my breasts in his hand he massaged them and then tweaked the nipples as he kept his erection buried in my vagina slowly grinding and pushing it deeper in me as an orgasm befell me. As my orgasm subsided, Braxton once again began to pound his cock in my pussy as my fingers dug into his back and I moaned, "You're so deep inside me. Oh God, it feels great!" Hearing that, Braxton thrust his penis even deeper than it had caused me to arch my back off the bed as I climaxed hard this time, my vaginal muscles tightening around Braxton's hardened ramrod as I screamed out loud, "I'm coming, oh god I am coming!" My pussy clamped around Braxton's cock so hard that it inhibited him from being able to withdraw it from my nether region. I could feel Braxton's cock twitching from the climax he had just felt from me and soon he was moaning, "Coming, oh God I am coming so hard!" Load after load of hot milky white semen poured from Braxton's cock buried deep within my nether regions. Collapsed on top of me, Braxton whispered in my ear, "I have never come so hard or so long as I just did." I couldn't help but smile.

Spent from our lovemaking, Braxton slowly got up and headed over to the table that Rhys had been sitting at watching us while he ate his sub. Standing up, Rhys gave Braxton a quick kiss before he climbed onto the bed with me, while Braxton sat down at the table and began to unwrap his sub. I couldn't help but smile at this display and fall even deeper in love with these two men. Sometimes things didn't need to be said between us, but instead, a look or a kiss said it all.

Rhys leaned over and kissed me our legs wrapping around each other as he held me close to his naked body. There was no hurriedness in our kissing, just slow and tender with a passion behind them. The warmth of his fingers on my back as I offered him my neck to lick and kiss. Between bated breaths, I mustered the word "please". My body had yet to come down off the orgasmic high that Braxton had given me and now I needed more.

"Not yet my love," Rhys said to me as his lips gently grazed against mine teasing me before he rolled on top of me pinning me beneath his muscular body. My hands caressed his body as my legs wrapped around his waist pulling him into me. I could feel his hardness probing my belly button, yet he was denying my pussy the cock she so was craving.

My fingers trailed toward Rhys' front and when they landed on his chest, I took his nipples in between my thumbs and forefingers and pinched them as my mouth bit his neck. "Oh fuck," he exclaimed as his cock grew even harder as he became more aroused. His kisses became more frenzied as his mouth pressed against mine his tongue pushing its way to my mouth.

With a free hand, Rhys positioned his ramrod at the entrance to my vagina and with a knee spread my legs further apart before slamming himself hard and deep causing me to scream, "Oh fuck," as he thrust his cock in me never fully pulling out. He was dominating me, reminding me he was in charge. My fingernails dug into his back as he pummeled my pussy with his hard cock.

As he fucked my pussy, he took my breast in his mouth and began to suck on it. I became unhinged and felt my body rise to orgasm between the sucking and pummeling he was doing to me. I needed this. I needed him to claim me once again as his and I craved to feel him shoot his spunk inside of me.

"Harder Rhys, please!" I begged as the thwap, thwap, thwap of skin on the skin could be heard through the moans we created. Obliging my command, Rhys pounded his cock harder and deeper inside of me, as I crescendoed and my juices coated his cock as he continued to pound me until he finally came deep inside of me.

Giving me a quick kiss on the lips Rhys got up from the bed and headed to the bathroom to take a shower while Braxton finished eating his sub and handed me mine. God, I was so hungry. Since coming back from Safe Haven I had yet to eat and now I was famished and my body was in dire need of the fuel, so I went over to the table that Braxton had handed to me and began to eat it. Right now, this sub was the most delicious thing I had ever eaten and nothing else mattered, not even sex. It takes a lot for me to say that something else matters more than sex, especially when I am sharing a bed with two of the most handsome men I have come to know and love, but right now I need sustenance.

As I sat at the table to eat my sub, Braxton got up kissed the top of my head, and headed to take a shower. I smiled because I knew that my lovers were going to have some fun in the shower together and I was perfectly fine with it. I was not in the mood to join them. I know crazy, right? How could I deny myself the pleasure of Rhys and Braxton? Oh, it was easy, I had had them several times since coming back from Safe Haven, so it was safe to allow them their own time together. Besides, a girl sometimes needs to have a nice hot shower all to herself without the interruptions of her lovers no matter how handsome and talented they may be. Oh, and food. Let us not forget the fact that I needed sustenance since I had not had anything to eat since we headed over to Safe Haven yesterday.

While I sat and enjoyed my sub, Rhys and Braxton were both in the bathroom together. I had to admit that the bathroom we had was quite large, and in fact, the shower could've accommodated all 3 of us together, but seeing as how I was the one to opt out of joining my lovers, I was going to allow for them to have their time together. I didn't need to be there with them to know that they were both naked, with the rainfall shower head streaming down over their muscular bodies, while the body shower jets allowed for the massage that they needed. I didn't need to be in there to know that they were entangled in an embrace and kissing each other. No, it was something that I instinctively knew because I had on occasion been a voyeur to their shower pleasures.

Rhys and Braxton were passionate lovers, and not just with me, but with each other. When they kissed each other the heat that erupted from their kissing needed to be extinguished. Factor in when they are wet from a shower and taking the simplest of activities like washing the other's body and turning it into a seduction that would make you wet just from watching it.

I took my time savoring my sub from last night as Braxton and Rhys took their time in the shower. When both emerged from the bathroom looking satisfied, clean, and refreshed I got up and gave each of them a quick kiss on the lips before heading into the bathroom to enjoy the time now by myself. I knew that Rhys and Braxton were up to something since today was my birthday, but I didn't press the subject. I knew that they were not going to divulge anything to me until they were ready to, and

I had to accept it, which was part of the reason that I had allowed them to have their time together in the shower. Now, I got to enjoy the quality time of being alone and relaxing before their plans were set in motion.

I took my time in the shower and when I got out, I took my time in getting ready. I had no idea what we were doing today except at some point we would be heading back to Safe Haven, so I had to be selective with my makeup and hair for the day. Clothes didn't matter too much since I always changed once I got to Safe Haven.

When I entered the bedroom both Rhys and Braxton were nowhere to be found. The only thing left for me was a box with a note attached which read, "*Dearest Mack. We will be back shortly, running an errand. In the meantime, please get dressed. XoXo. Rhys & Braxton.*"

I couldn't help but smile at the note because both men were busy doing something that involved celebrating my birthday. Opening the box, I pulled out the most elegant strapless black floral satin dress that hit just above the knee with a slit going up my left leg to mid-thigh. The dress was form-fitted and fit me like a glove. Also in the box was a pair of lace-up platform sandals with a 4" stiletto heal in black. Seeing this outfit left me with more questions than answers. I was perplexed. I had no iota as to what these men were up to only that I was going to have to trust them.

By the time I was dressed, Braxton had returned to the hotel room, but Rhys was not with him.

"Where's Rhys?" I asked Braxton my face showing my confusion.

Chuckling Braxton replied, "He's somewhere waiting for us. He wanted me to come get you." Holding his hand out to me he said, "If you would, please follow me." I placed my hand in Braxton's and allowed him to lead the way to our next stop.

Arriving outside, Braxton led me to a Rolls Royce Phantom in the deepest sapphire blue color I had ever seen. A chauffeur had opened the door and Braxton helped me in before sidling up next to me. With the door closed, I looked at Braxton shocked, unable to find the right words to say so I just sat there in silence.

A short ride later we arrived at a gated house. It wasn't so much a house but a small mansion. Getting out of the car with Braxton, I followed him up the front steps still not saying anything just yet. I was starting to wonder though, whose house we were at and what were Braxton and Rhys up to.

⌒○ Chapter 5

As Braxton led the way through the house, I was captivated by the elegance it exuded. I honestly could not imagine who owned this luxurious place, but I was curious to find out. I knew better than to ask Braxton any questions though because he wouldn't divulge any details until it was time.

Before long, Braxton led me to a pair of oak doors that were closed. When he opened them up and ushered me inside, there stood Rhys along with Bella, Eros, and Cassidy. A table with silver and gold balloons was pushed up against a wall with presents wrapped on them. A longer, matching table was set with floral centerpieces. Finally, a small table with a birthday cake that said, "Happy Birthday Mackenzie & Braxton" sat in front of a large picture window that overlooked the backyard.

I was shocked. Here was my BDSM family coming together to celebrate our birthdays. I had always been under the impression that we would come to Safe Haven to play, and celebrate our birthdays as a thruple but never in my wildest dreams could I have imagined that we would be at someone's place celebrating our birthdays.

"Oh, you guys!" I exclaimed. "What is all this?"

Smiling, Rhys said, "Oh, this is the birthday celebration for both you and Braxton that we had planned. I had to lie to Braxton about the party and tell him it was just for you, but it was for a good reason. "

Smiling, Bella looked at both Braxton and me and said, "Rhys said he wanted to celebrate at Safe Haven, but when Dimitri suggested throwing a surprise party for you both at his house, this is what we came up with."

By now both Braxton and I were standing there shocked. Braxton, who is always calm, cool, and collected was flustered. I have to admit it was nice to see him flustered, and if I dare say so, even sexy.

Walking over to Braxton, Rhys handed him a drink, a whiskey I assumed, and kissed him on the mouth as he said, "Happy birthday handsome." Then he turned to me, bought me a glass of sangria, and kissed me as he said, "Happy birthday beautiful."

"Thank you," I said. "This is not what I was expecting."

Dimitri smiled. "Good, I am glad. This is going to be a fun-filled day, and yes, there will be time to play as well."

"Yes," Bella said. "Safe Haven might be closed, but trust me, Dimitri's place is equipped for some fun."

Braxton turned and looked at Bella shocked at what he just heard. "Wait, did you say you closed Safe Haven?"

"Yes darling, Safe Haven has been closed for personnel training," she chuckled. "Both you and Mackenzie are well worth closing the place for, to celebrate your birthdays in style."

"Bella," I began. "I don't know what to say except, thank you." I had no idea what might be in store for us, but now knowing that we were in Dimitri's home, I knew that it would be interesting.

"Why don't we all take a seat at the table," Dimitri said. "Food first, and fun afterward."

I raised an eye to Dimitri and saw something in his eyes that many might have missed, but after yesterday, I knew Dimitri had something special planned for me that would not involve anyone else. Seeing my look, he nodded to me as he held up his glass and said, "A toast to Mackenzie and Braxton. Happy birthday and enjoy everything that today has to offer."

Following our food, we all sat around for a bit laughing and joking before Bella suggested that Braxton and I open our birthday gifts. Honestly, I was happy just being here and able to celebrate with some very special people, gifts were not needed, but everyone went ahead anyway.

The first gift I opened was from Cassidy and Bella and I knew that it was going to be interesting. Both of these women were impeccable masters and anything that they gave me would be eye-catching. Cassidy and Bella gave me a vinyl and mesh 2-piece open cup bra and panty with an open caged back with grommets that ran along the ass cheeks in black; a black leather crop; black thigh-high leather lace-up boots with a 6 ¼" solid brass heel; and a black leather Jezebel collar with pearls. I was already smiling just imagining myself wearing this outfit.

"Mackenzie, every good Mistress needs an outfit to exude her status as such, and Cassidy and I both agreed it was time to take you under our wing to become the best Mistress that you can be," Bella said to me.

Shocked I could only muster, "Really?"

"Really," Cassidy replied to me beaming. "You have come so far in 9 months, something we don't typically see, but with you, there is something special." Getting up I sauntered over to Bella and Cassidy and gave each of them a hug and kiss before sitting back down. It was very heartwarming to have both women say that they would like to start working more on my status as a Mistress.

Next, I opened up a gift from Dimitri. He got me an intricately patterned leather "O" ring collar which I was completely shocked by because I had not expected this from him.

"Mackenzie," Dimitri began. "Do you understand what is behind the meaning of this collar?"

"I – I think so," I stuttered. "It means that I am your slave now once I put it on."

"In essence, yes darling you are now mine. But let me preface this with the understanding that I have asked for permission from Bella, Braxton, and Rhys to allow me to make this claim on you."

"Ok," I just said as I sat there looking at him.

"Oh, Mackenzie relax," Rhys laughed. "Dimitri doesn't typically take on a claim for a slave of his own, but we all have noticed that he tends to be the best Master when it comes to you and your training. We all understand that the Master/Slave role is a very special one, and one that we felt was worth it for you."

I could feel the heat in my cheeks, and I knew I was blushing. I wasn't blushing because of embarrassment, but more because secretly I was happy that Dimitri had laid ownership over me when it came to BDSM. I thoroughly enjoyed what he could do to me and my body and was going to look forward to more of it. Add in the fact that Bella and Cassidy would be taking me on to hone my skills as a Mistress, I was excited for things to come. So, I walked over to Dimitri with the collar in my hand, knelt in front of him, and rested my head in his lap allowing him to secure the collar around my neck. By doing this I showed everyone that I was accepting of his collar and welcomed him as my Master. While it might not have been the time to do so, I felt that it was best that I allowed it to transpire now rather than later.

With the collar secured around my neck, I rose to my feet and kissed Dimitri on each cheek. "Thank you, Master," I said as I went back to my seat next to Braxton and Rhys.

Up next, Rhys came over and handed Braxton and each a small box and said, "I love you both. Happy birthday," and gave each one of us a kiss. Opening up our boxes, Braxton and I both noticed we both got identical rings that had the BDSM triskelion with our initials etched on the inside of the band. Both Braxton and I looked at each other for a moment before we slipped the ring on our fingers and then we saw Rhys take his out of his pocket and slip it on his finger as well.

The alcohol was flowing but so were the jokes and laughter that came with it. Braxton and I had gone through all of our presents now, except for one that Braxton handed to me. "Mack love, this is from both of us. Happy birthday precious." I opened up the tiny box to reveal a heart necklace with an infinity symbol inside of it. The heart was encrusted with micro-pave pink Tourmaline while the infinity symbol had micro-pave navy-blue Spinel.

"Oh Rhys, Braxton this is lovely. Thank you," I said as Braxton removed the collar and put the necklace on me.

"Now, these stones have special meaning," began Rhys. "The blue Spinel symbolizes calmness, wisdom, and protection, while the pink

Tourmaline symbolizes passion, love, healing, and awareness. These are all qualities you possess."

I was shocked. These guys had gone ahead and made sure that they got me something meaningful to wear every day. "Thank you both so much," I said as I took a moment to kiss each one of them.

The three of us were in a serious and committed relationship that we had to hide from the outside world because many didn't understand it. Many people didn't want to understand it or even consider that someone could love more than one person at a time and be in a committed relationship with both people simultaneously. These rings were a symbol of our relationship and love for each other. By far, I think that this was the most precious gift that Braxton and I could've received. Plus, it allowed us to hold a piece of each other without the misconceptions placed on us by the world around us.

There would have been a time when I would have been apprehensive about this sort of get-together, but now, I am dare I say it – excited. Quite honestly, I was looking forward to setting some scenes with everyone but especially Dimitri. Dimitri was a great master and probably the best one for me since the more I got involved with scenes the more I was discovering the SM (sadomasochist) part of myself. Dimitri or Eros in the BDSM world was a sadomasochist and his dungeon as we all tend to call it, definitely reflected it. While most people would be uncomfortable with him, I felt right at home with him, and having the ability to be his official submissive was quite exciting for me.

Today was about letting all my inhibitions go and just allowing for whatever happens to happen. This was a get-together with people who understood you and enjoyed you and I planned to make the most of it. I was excited because I was going to start to learn the art of becoming a Mistress from Bella and Cassidy, and I would get to explore myself as a submissive with Eros in greater depth. Now, none of this was going to happen overnight, but this would be a gradual learning experience, to begin the lessons outside of Safe Haven was something unique in and of itself.

Yes, we could have gone ahead and cut the cake, however, Bella had suggested that we split up and have a little fun together first and then reconvene for some cake. Rhys, Braxton, and Eros would spend time together while Bella, Cassidy, and I would do the same. While I didn't laugh out loud, secretly I was hysterical laughing because I knew that the guys while they could play together, preferred not to because Eros was a tad bit too sadomasochist for both of them. Oh, let's not forget that all three men were Masters in their own right so finding a way to play together tended to get interesting for them. Still, I wish I could have been a fly on the wall that got to witness all three men together.

Chapter 6

Bella led Cassidy and me to a room that was tastefully decorated yet still portrayed the essence of BDSM as well. This was going to be a lesson for me, one that I was honored to receive. While I had been with both Bella and Cassidy together in the past, things would be different as they worked with me to make me a better Mistress. Up until now, most of what I had done had been as a submissive, although I was not a submissive nor a dominant, but a switch. The fact that I was a switch allowed for me to be both, and as such, this was important for me, so that I could better understand the BDSM world and what it meant for me when I was in the Mistress' role.

"In the world of BDSM, the Mistress or Master has a very important role that for many, fail at," Cassidy began. "As a Mistress you are responsible for your submissive. You are responsible for their well-being, their desires, and their needs. Most of all it is about the power you have over your submissive while maintaining safe, sane, and consensual practices."

"More than that, however, it is about communication, trust, and the safe word. Know, that while the bulk of power is in your hands, your submissive has power too – that safe word. Knowing that you respect your submissive or slave is a critical aspect of the master/slave relationship, one that should never be taken for granted," Bella added.

Just hearing all this made me stop and think about the Dominant/Submissive roles versus the Master/Slave. "Wait, I began," taking a breath before I continued, "can we talk a little more about the differences between the Dominant/Submissive versus the Master/Slave roles? I mean, I know that there is a difference, but I feel like we should define it a bit more."

Bella smiled and let out a haughty laugh. "Oh, my dear, only now do you ask after you have said yes to Eros as being his slave?"

"Well, I- um," I stuttered. "Yes." I managed to muster out.

"Relax Mackenzie," Bella said. "I know you know there's a difference, but now that we are working on your potential as a Mistress, it was a fair question to ask. Many don't ever think of the Master/Slave and Dominant/Submissive roles as being different, but they are in fact. Do you have any idea what that might be?"

"Rules," I said.

"To an extent," Cassidy said, "but the difference is control. As a submissive, you have the safe word, and the ability to set limits. The slave for all purposes has given up that control and you are essentially owned by the Master. You don't question what the Master is telling you -you just do it."

"Ah, I get it." I couldn't help but smile. "Up until now, I have been the submissive in our scenes, but now with Eros, I will be the slave."

"Pretty much, unless he decides to give you some sort of authority, like a safe word," Bella said. "The fact he asked us for permission to ask you to be his slave says a lot since he's not the type to ever want one, but he did. Now, you both will have to discover your Master/Slave relationship and what that means to you both, how you deal with it when apart, etc."

"In your opinion Bella, do you think this is all going to be easier or harder on me since I am a switch?"

"Mackenzie, I wish I knew, but I don't. You have surprised us all at every turn and have been able to master what has been thrown at you. You're in a relationship with two very dominant Masters, and both have said that you have managed to hold your own in the relationship, even dominating them sometimes without even knowing you are doing it," Bella said.

"Bella's right," Cassidy said. "When I talked with Braxton, he told me that he's seen you just naturally take charge and not even blink an eye when the three of you are together intimately. Now, we need to make it so that when you are in the Mistress role, you are being just that, dominating, caring, and consensual and when you are the slave, you are obedient."

"So how do we make me a better dominant? A better Mistress?" I was genuinely interested in the answer to it all.

"Communication is first and foremost," Bella acknowledged. "Sit down, talk about the dos and don'ts, and figure out what your submissive is willing to do or wants to do."

"Yes, definitely communication, and with that communication comes your aftercare," Cassidy said assuredly. "Sometimes, your submissive might need something from you following whatever scene it is you did that you might be unaware they needed. Communication is key and just asking that person if there is anything they might need from you, is what will set you apart from some of the others."

Hearing both of them talk made me realize just why they were excellent Mistresses and just how lucky I was to be under their tutelage. As much as this lesson was important, I still wanted to be with both Bella and Cassidy. My desire to be with them both sexually was something I longed for since I first had. Together they awakened something inside me that I didn't know I needed, and today, I need it.

Almost as if she could read my mind, Bella took both Cassidy and me by the hand and led us to the massive bed that sat in the center of the room. "Come, ladies, let's enjoy the pleasure of our bodies naked together and feast on our carnal pleasures," she smiled.

Each of us slowly undressed each move like the game of seduction yet there was no need to seduce, we all wanted the same thing, pleasure. We wanted to feast on our bodies together and we knew that titillating fantasy men think about when they hear of women satiating their needs without a man would drive the most normal man to pieces, but here in the world of BDSM, this was normal. You could play out your biggest fantasy and no one would think less of you.

I was lucky enough to have men who knew how to satiate my every need, but yet I would be amiss if I didn't add Bella and Cassidy into the mix. These ladies were masters as well, and I had had the pleasure of them once before and found myself longing for another moment together with just them – no men involved. It is quite surprising how the world of BDSM can open you up to new and pleasurable experiences if you just allow yourself the freedom to do so. I am so glad Rhys took me to Safe Haven six months ago because had he not I would be missing out on so much that for me is my normal today. I wouldn't have Braxton in my life. I wouldn't be here with Bella and Cassidy, nor would I have Eros in my life. My life is the better because of it all.

All three of us now naked climbed onto the bed and I was sandwiched between Cassidy and Bella waiting for my lessons to begin in earnest. "For your first lesson as a Mistress, we are going to teach you about queening. I feel like queening is the penultimate with a dominant and submissive because this is allowing the submissive some power because they have been given the power to pleasure you as you sit on their face," Cassidy said as she climbed her way up the bed like the minx she was and sat on my face. While she sat on my face, she didn't smother me, but I could smell her lovely scent as it wafted through my nostrils and I couldn't help myself, I had to taste her.

With my tongue, I slowly licked around her bud and slowly kissed it. She tasted divine. Oh, I had tasted Cassidy before but never like this, this was something else entirely and it was provocative. The more I licked, kissed, and sucked her clit the wetter she became, and her moans increased. This was definitely a turn-on for me, and I could feel myself getting wet down there, but unfortunately, there was no one to satisfy my needs. What was Bella doing, I had no idea since I couldn't see anything other than the backside of Cassidy.

Slowly I nipped at Cassidy's lips as her wetness grew and my tongue flicked incessantly in her clit and hitting her G-spot. "Oh fuck," I could hear her exclaim as I continued to assault her pussy with everything I had. "I'm so close," she could be heard saying through breaths. It didn't bother me though because I was enjoying this, realizing my potential and savoring the moment. As I kissed Cassidy's clit again, I felt the beginning of her orgasm, so I changed to my tongue and slightly grazed her lips with my teeth, causing her to climax and spurt her juices all over my face as I lapped them up best I could. "Oh God, Oh God, fuck that's it," she moaned.

Once done, Cassidy got up off of my face and handed me a towel to wipe myself with, before collapsing down next to me. "Fuck," she said, "that was impressive Mackenzie. Thank you."

Rolling over I kissed her on her mouth, our lips parting to allow for our tongues to dart in and out, playing with each other along the way.

"Mackenzie get on all fours and straddle Cassidy," Bella ordered. Barely breaking from my kisses with Cassidy, I straddled her as I got on all fours as Bella instructed while I waited for what would come next.

Cassidy broke from our kiss, grabbed one of my breasts, and placed the nipple in her mouth, her tongue gently rolling over it, gliding around it, playing with it. "Mm, that's nice," I moaned as pleasure coursed through my body, but I knew I needed more. As Cassidy continued to do that, I felt Bella's hands on my hips and repositioning them slightly as she gently thrust the dildo into my pussy causing me to gasp in delight. "Oh, fuck, yeah, that's it, please," I begged.

Bella was fucking my pussy from behind with the dildo as Cassidy continued to suck on my breasts, occasionally biting one. The pace wasn't frenzied as much as it was needed, and the more my pussy got pounded by the dildo the more heightened my orgasms became until I unleashed the torrent of cum soaking the bed in the process.

"Fuck," I exclaimed. "I needed that."

Bella laughed. "You were magnificent Mackenzie. I am so glad we could satisfy you," she said as she kissed me on the mouth, my lips parting to allow her tongue entrance to my mouth. Her kiss was passionate, enticing making me want her even more than I had already.

I had everything I needed at my disposal, I just had to do something about it, so I grabbed the handcuffs that were strapped to the bed and cuffed Bella's wrists in them as Cassidy tied Bella's ankles to the bed. Laying there naked and cuffed to the bed, Bella was the epitome of a goddess, and I was going to enjoy her body now with Cassidy.

With a feather in her hand, Cassidy teased Bella's pussy, while I sucked on her breast. Bella's moans of ecstasy echoed throughout the room as her body writhed on the bed. Here was a woman who could control herself, but right now, she was far from being in control and I was enjoying the fact that she was losing it.

Cassidy and I slowly teased Bella's body, between kisses on her lips, nips at her neck to eating her pussy out, all of which made her come undone even more than she had already. When I strapped on the dildo, she had used to fuck me with and rammed it into her hole, her body arched up off the bed as she screamed in delight. As I rammed Bella's pussy with the dildo, Cassidy sat on Bella's face queening her. As she ate Cassidy out, Bella moaned, "Oh I am so close to coming!" We were relentless, we loved her body, and made it come several times before we untied her and allowed her freedom where we cuddled together for a bit before Bella noticed the time and told us, "We should get dressed, it is almost dinner time."

Slowly we dressed and headed back out towards the dining room where we met up with Braxton, Eros, and Rhys for dinner.

Chapter 7

Eros had outdone himself when it came to dinner. Luckily for us, we all knew that as much food as there was being provided, we knew that we would burn through those calories. The night was still young, and we were all spending the night here.

To start with, Eros served us Tirokroketes, or fried cheese balls, followed by Kleftiko, or a slow-roasted lamb with potatoes and vegetables, and then for dessert the birthday cake that we had yet to have. To be quite honest, the birthday cake seemed out of place with the Greek dinner we were having, yet once we cut into it, Dimitri surprised us and kept with the theme and served us a traditional Greek orange cake and a cup of Greek coffee. Up until now, I had not thought much about Dimitri's Greek heritage, yet tonight at dinner, I was thinking more about the man and not the Master.

Following dessert, it was time to play once again. It was a given I was going to be with Eros since he had claimed me as his slave and we had a lot of stuff we needed to work out where that relationship was concerned. More importantly, I was excited because I thoroughly enjoyed my time with him.

I was one of the few women let alone people that can handle the sadomasochist that Eros was. Somehow, Eros managed to do things to me and make me feel things I never expected to feel and I loved it. When I am with him it is a journey of self-exploration into my deepest, darkest desires that I didn't realize I had.

Taking my hand, Eros led me down the hall and unlocked a door that had been locked. Once we were behind the doors, he looked at me and smiled. "Mackenzie, my beautiful slave welcome to my bedroom. You are the first person to ever step inside."

His master bedroom was a deep crimson color with a hint of a greyish pattern to it exuding masculinity and elegance. His king-sized bed reflected his personality; it was a four-poster bed made in black bronze steel tubing with restraint hoops in all four corners as well as at mattress height. Additional restraint hoops ran along the bottom edge of bedframe. At the foot of the bed sat a steel bench that matched the bed topped with a black leather cushion. Nightstands in black bronze flanked both sides of the bed as well. His bed was fitted with black satin play sheets, pillowcases, and a comforter in black with the BDSM triskelion in white and grey handcuffs attached to the triskelion.

"Dimitri- I mean Eros erm I mean-," I stuttered as he laughed.

"Relax my dear," he said as he pulled me to him. "Right now, we are just Dimitri and Mackenzie, and we will discover whatever pleasures we want to discover tonight. No master/slave although we will talk about that some and maybe set a few rules up for the future. Deal?"

I couldn't help it; I had to lead with my emotions after what he just said to me. I brought my mouth to his and kissed him with a savageness, unlike anything he'd seen from me before. There was something in me that needed him, longed for him, and would not be satisfied until I had him and I knew he sensed it as well.

Quickly we undressed the other as we continued to kiss. In between kisses, he told me to wrap my legs around his waist and my arms around his neck. Listening to what he asked of me, I did it and there Dimitri effortlessly carried me to the massive bed in the center of the room and laid down on top of me.

"Mine," he growled as he plowed his hard cock into my wet pussy.

"Yes, yours," I said breathlessly as I arched off the bed as he drove his cock deep inside of me.

The scent of sandalwood, coffee, and a hint of spice assaulted my senses as he pounded his hardness in and out of me. Together our bodies moved in sync like a metronome assisting a musician with their tempo.

"Oh fuck!" I exclaimed as Dimitri rammed his cock in and out of my snatch as I gripped the bedsheets in my fists.

"So wet for me already," he claimed as he pounded me quicker and harder while I entwined my legs in his pushing him closer to me.

I knew he desired me but more importantly, I knew he needed release just as much as I needed it. As I climaxed, he continued to thrust deep inside of me his cock throbbing for release.

"Mm, Dimitri," I moaned as he continued to fuck me. "Harder please!" I begged of him.

"Fuck, I am going to come," he exclaimed as he thrust in me and my pussy quivered excitedly squeezing his cock until he erupted spilling all he had deep within me.

As he lay there on top of me, his cock still buried within me, he kissed me passionately. Our mouths met parting to allow our tongues to explore. My fingers trailed down his back lightly but just enough to cause him chills on his hot skin.

Finally withdrawing his cock from my snatch, Dimitri lay next to me and wrapped an arm over my body as he spooned me.

"Happy birthday my love," he whispered to me as he continued to hold me.

Turning my head slightly to face him I smiled, "Thank you," as I brought my mouth up to his and kissed him. It was the first time he referred to me as "my love" but it warmed me. I knew I was starting to develop feelings for this man.

There we lay together for a bit, nothing else being said, no kissing just Dimitri's arm wrapped around my naked body. His warmth felt good.

"Dimitri," I said but paused to think for a moment how I wanted to phrase what I wanted to say next.

"Hmm, yes?"

"Why did you decide to take a slave now after never taking one?"

"It's a story I will tell you about another day, but know that I did it because I could tell that there was something developing between us. I knew it was the only way we could safely explore what was happening between us without the constant intrusion at Safe Haven. Was I wrong to do so?"

"No, you made the correct call. I have never been happier than to be your slave and have time with you without those intrusions."

"Well, Mackenzie dear, you being my slave also allows us a little more freedom to do stuff outside of Safe Haven since it is something expected from us."

"What do you mean?" I wasn't sure exactly what he was trying to say, but it almost sounded like we could date each other outside of Safe Haven. Was that what he was trying to say? I did need him to clarify that for me.

"Well, part of the master/slave relationship is carving time outside of playing to discuss any potential issues either one of us might have. Plus, it allows me to show you off to the public too. Most importantly, we can drop the pretense of master/slave that we have to have at Safe Haven. It allows us to just be Dimitri and Mackenzie."

"So, what you are saying is that it will afford us the privacy we need to learn about the intricate feelings we are both potentially having for the other. Am I right?"

"Yes, very much so."

I couldn't help but smile. Hearing that he was developing feelings for me but wanted to explore them outside of Safe Haven was the best thing I could have been told. We had other people to consider, so we both knew we couldn't just declare our feelings and then be wrong about them.

"But enough talk about our slave/master relationship. Tonight, I want to savor every inch of your naked body. I want to drown in your ecstasy."

I let out a hearty laugh. "Dimitri, are you getting all mushy on me?"

Scoffing he looked at me, his eyes wild with promise, "No, I am being a man who wants to enjoy his beautiful and sexy lover."

"Only if you promise some bondage as well," I said grinning.

"Oh, I promise I will fulfill that desire," he said as he rolled on top of me kissing me his tongue in my mouth showing his urgent desire as the last of the coffee aroma emanated from his breath. I couldn't wait to explore the night with him, not as anything more than his lover.

⛓ Chapter 8

I couldn't believe it, here I was spending the night with Dimitri in his bed and he had just told me that I was the first person ever to step into his bedroom. This was huge because he was involved with Bella, yet it made me also curious as to why he's never had her here in his room. While I wanted to ask him, I also knew that now was not the time to do it. Right now, we were free to be alone. When I left with Dimitri Rhys, Braxton, Cassidy, and Bella were all pairing off, but most likely would swap partners at some point if I knew the four of them like I thought I did. I could only assume we were being left alone Dimitri had claimed me as his slave, they had all agreed that we had to establish our dos and don'ts and whatnot so they just figured that we would need the night. Yes, they were right, we did have to work on the rules of the slave/master relationship, but right now, we just wanted the chance to be together without that stigma attached to it.

In the world of BDSM, there is no black and white. The standard rules of sex don't apply because it is not just plain vanilla sex once you start factoring in the fetishes and kinks. You rarely end up with 2 sadomasochists together let alone be in a relationship outside of that world. Now, here we both were and had been giving blessings from everyone that mattered. What I don't think they were planning on is for us to have developed feelings, but here Dimitri and I were with the possibility of having feelings of more than a sub/dom or slave/master. Maybe we have these feelings and we play so well together because Dimitri is a dominant and I am a switch, so it allows for me to be both a submissive and a dominant. In any event, having the chance to discover what was going on between us was special.

"Stay here a minute I need to get something from my dresser," he said to me as he quickly got up and retrieved a small box. When he climbed back in bed, he handed me the box and said, "Happy birthday Mackenzie. This is your actual present."

Questioning Dimitri now, I looked at him and asked him, "But why didn't you give it to me when we were all together?"

"Mackenzie, open the present please," he firmly but sweetly said to me.

Opening the black velvet box, it revealed an anklet but not just any anklet; it was a stainless-steel heart anklet with an "O" to signify the submissive bond, and dangling from the "O" a micro heart dangling from it. "Oh, Dimitri! It is exquisite. Thank you!" I said as I put the anklet on before I leaned over and kissed him on the mouth.

As we continued to kiss, I climbed on top of Dimitri, straddling him. I could already feel him starting to get erect again. The only problem with being in his bedroom and not his lair at Safe Haven was I didn't know where he kept all of the BDSM paraphernalia so I was going to have to ask him.

"Sir, where do you keep your BDSM stuff?" I sweetly asked him between kisses.

"Hmm, I like it when you call me sir. Maybe I will show you since you are such a good girl," he teasingly said to me.

"Please sir," I responded. "I would be honored if you were to show me where everything is kept." I knew we both didn't have to acknowledge our status as slave/master tonight, but when I just instinctively called him sir, things shifted between us.

Calling Dimitri sir turned him on. He was sporting an erection now, and I could feel myself getting wet. Seeing him hard was a turn-on for me.

"Were you looking for something specific slave?"

"Yes sir, I wanted to see your cock ring."

"Very well," he said. "If you get off of me, I will show you where everything is kept."

I quickly got off of Dimitri and followed him to his massive closet where not only his regular clothes hung, but his different BDSM clothing was. There, in the closet, he had a dresser in the center which he indicated was designated BDSM toys.

Oh, my goodness! I couldn't believe it; I was standing at a dresser that contained BDSM toys for both men and women. This man was truly a master, yet it made me want to question why all of this if he'd never allowed another person into his sanctuary until me.

I could hear Dimitri chuckling behind me. "Do you like what you see Mackenzie?"

I turned to him and smiled, "Oh yes, very much. So many ideas. So many different things we could use on each other."

"I'm so glad. I promise we will explore every last item together. But is there a cock ring you like?"

"Yes, give me a moment and I will join you in bed. I just want to pick the right one."

"God you are so sexy. I can't wait to have my dick inside your wet pussy."

"Good, because I can't wait for it to be inside of me."

Once he left me alone to peruse his collection, I felt like I was a kid in a candy shop unsure of what to choose because there were so many options to be had. After picking up and handling the cock rings I ended up choosing a vibrating one that would not only provide stimulation for him but clitoral stimulation for me.

There on his king-sized bed, he laid like a Greek god and it turned me on. Just seeing him lying there patiently for me to return caused my pussy to get wet. This man had one hell of an effect on every inch of my body.

"Did you find what you wanted beautiful?" he asked me.

"I did. Thank you." I said as I crawled slowly on the bed toward him, cock ring in the palm of my hand.

Under his breath, I could hear him growl at me. "Fuck, you are so sexy like that."

I loved to hear him tell me how sexy I was, but right now I wanted nothing more than to pleasure him, taste him in my mouth. Crawling up to cock, I stopped and took it in a hand and started to stroke him while I gently massaged his balls with my other hand. I was enjoying feeling his largeness in my hand as I stroked it.

"Mm mm. Yeah, that feels nice," he moaned as I continued to stroke him.

I was far from done; I was just beginning. As he continued to grow harder as I stroked him, I wrapped my mouth around his cock and began to suck and lick his cock. My slurping mingled with moans from Dimitri as I continued to suck him, lick him When I removed my mouth from around his cock and gently kissed the tip of it before blowing on it, his cock jumped in delight pre-cum starting to form from it as well.

"Fuck!" he exclaimed. "I'm not sure if I am going to last much longer. This feels insanely perfect."

I smiled knowing I was getting to him. It was time to take my plan to the next level. I once again took him in my mouth and sucked him for a moment, getting his cock as wet as it could while he continued to moan in ecstasy. With the cock ring in my hand, I removed my mouth and slid the cock ring onto his engorgement and then started it up.

As the vibrations from the cock ring occurred, his cock was getting even harder now. Stradling his cock, I slowly lowered myself onto it as he slid between my velvety folds.

"Mm. Fuck!" was all he managed to get out as I started to rock back and forth with his cock impaled in me.

Grabbing ahold of my hips he continued to pound me our hips rocking back and forth as he slid in and out of me. Leaning down towards his mouth, the angle of his protrusion changed hitting that sweet spot in me causing my body to quiver as orgasm racked me.

Our mouths met with wet greedy need. Our tongues flitted back and forth as he continued to hold onto my hips and pound my clit until he bottomed out deep inside of me. There he held himself for a moment before he slid himself almost out before ramming me hard and fast.

"Oh yeah, that's it," I moaned as he continued to fuck me hard and fast. I was wet and getting wetter as he did this. I couldn't keep track of how many orgasms he had gotten from me by this point, but it felt good.

"I'm close baby!" he yelled as he held my hips down and pounded his cock hard into me screaming as I came, gushing all over his cock as he exploded deep inside of me, coating my walls with his semen.

Climbing off of him, Dimitri removed the cock ring and placed it on the nightstand beside the bed before wrapping me in his arms and kissing me. The smell of sex permeated the air, but it didn't bother us because we were far from being over. The night was still young and we had all the time in the world to discover ourselves outside of the sub/dom or master/slave relationship.

I wrapped my legs around Dimitri's. My nails trailed down his back as we kissed. My desire for him was growing and I needed him more than I needed to breathe at this moment. His fingers entwined in my hair. We were taking our time, enjoying the moment. I couldn't tell you how long we stayed wrapped in each other's arms kissing before anything else transpired.

"Close your eyes for a moment, my dear," he lovingly whispered to me.

I couldn't help but obey so I did as he requested closed my eyes and waited for him to tell me what to do next.

"No peaking," he firmly said to me.

"I'm not," I responded.

With my eyes closed I had no idea what he was up to, but I knew that I trusted him. Pinning my hands above my head with a firm hand, Dimitri was taking control, dominating me, but I wanted him to. Still closed, I couldn't see what he was doing, but I felt what he was doing.

Not only was he getting erect, but he was also handcuffing me to the bed. Both wrists were secured above my head. My eyes remained closed as I felt him get off of me and the bed shift. I wasn't sure what he was doing, but I could only expect that I was going to enjoy it; he had after all already handcuffed my wrists.

"Keep your eyes closed," he said.

I giggled. "I am. I am trying to be patient, sir." I couldn't help but add the sir in there since I knew that it turned him on.

Dimitri took hold of my left leg snapped an ankle cuff on it and then moved onto my right leg doing the same. Here I was on his bed, spread eagle and it was hot- I was getting aroused just thinking about the things he could do to me while I was bound to his bed.

"You may open your eyes now my dear," he said as his mouth crushed mine with wet, sloppy kisses. Blood was rushing through his body and down to his cock which sat outside of my vagina that was getting wet with need. I was enjoying this. I was enjoying being bound to the bed and unable to do anything.

Slowly Dimitri's tongue trailed down my neck towards my breasts. Taking a nipple in his mouth he began to play with one breast as he massaged it and then switched to ravish attention on the other one. A whimper escaped my lips as he lavished attention on my breasts before he continued to lick and kiss me down my stomach until he reached my clit.

There he buried his face in my nether region which was drenched from our lovemaking already and once again getting wet from arousal. With delicate fingers, Dimitri parted the folds of my clitoris as he placed a kiss on it before his tongue probed my entrance.

Unable to grab onto the sheets, I could only moan, "Oh god, yeah." As he continued to lick and suck my pussy. He just continued to ravish attention to my pussy with his mouth as the feeling of ecstasy overwhelmed my senses and I was gushing fluid from my womanhood from the orgasm that he had been able to create with just his mouth.

"Oh fuck, that was nice," I said as I came down off of the orgasm.

"Good, glad you are enjoying it, but I am far from done," he grinned as his mouth pressed against mine with desire. I could taste my sweet juices on his lips as they brushed against mine and our tongues danced the rumba.

Meanwhile, his cock was hard and erect pressing against my opening waiting. I could even feel the pre-cum dripping from his penis but was unable to do anything about it since I was handcuffed to the bed. All I could do was tell him, "Please take me. I need to feel your hardness buried deep inside of me, pounding me, claiming me."

"Soon," he said between kisses.

Leaning up to meet his mouth one last time I instead turned and bit the side of his neck. When I did this, he let out a gasp of delight while his cock slid inside of my pussy.

Feeling his cock slide inside of me I couldn't help but moan with delight as I thrust my pelvis up to his and started to grind against him, drawing his cock deeper inside of me. The slapping of our naked bodies sounded in the silent bedroom as Dimitri would remove his cock and then slam it hard and fast deep inside me. At the same time, he placed his hands around my throat and began to squeeze choking me. The pleasure that coursed through my veins was overwhelming as orgasm wracked my body.

Dimitri continued with quick rapid thrusts of his cock in and out of my pussy as I came once again and soon, he was coming, hot milky white semen shooting out and covering my cervix. When he was finished, he quickly undid the handcuffs and ankle cuffs and we lay together once again naked.

Chapter 9

As we lay together, we both must've dozed off because when I awoke, the sun had set completely and the moon was high in the sky. I couldn't help but wonder what time it was, but I also didn't want to wake him up so I just laid there in his embrace and smiled. I couldn't help being content with everything that was happening between us.

Just then Dimitri started to stir to life. "Hey handsome," I whispered.

"Mm, hey beautiful," he said stroking my cheek as he leaned into me and gently kissed me on the mouth. "How long have you been awake?"

"Not long," I said kissing him back. As I kissed him, I could feel his arousal pressing against my stomach. I couldn't help but chuckle and say to him, "I see someone else is awake."

Dimitri rolled over on top of me and pinned me to the bed, his cock positioned at the entrance to my clit but not inserting it just yet. In his deep husky voice, he looked at me and said, "Mackenzie you have no idea what you do to me, do you? Do you know you're the first woman that could ever get me hard, make me come, and then immediately get all hard again without trying to?"

Looking him straight in the eyes I told him, "Then claim me as yours. Take me and make me yours again Dimitri."

That was all he needed to hear before he thrust his ramrod deep into my pussy and then started to grind against me hard and fast as I wrapped my legs around his body tightly pulling him down onto me, driving him even further into my hole.

"Oh, fuck Mackenzie, you feel wonderful," he moaned as his cock continued to plunge in and out of my pussy.

"Oh yeah, that's it. Harder please," I begged as he continued to thrust his erection into my pussy while I shuddered from an orgasm.

As he continued to pound me, he kissed my neck his teeth gently grazing the skin as I could feel the warmth of his breath through his kiss. The kiss was sensual and sent chills throughout my body even though we were both hot and sweaty from the amount of sex we were having. I couldn't help it; he was driving me crazy in the best way possible and I was close to coming once again.

"Faster. I am so close," I supplicated as the muscles in my belly tightened with anticipation of the oncoming orgasm.

Deep inside me he thrust his cock and stilled before withdrawing it from me and forcing it back into me until he bottomed out inside of me. As he did this my body climaxed and I moaned loudly, "Oh god, yes! I am coming!"

As I said this, he couldn't help himself and exploded coating my pussy with his jizz. "Mm, fuck. Yeah. Oh god, yes, I'm coming!" he bellowed.

When he was done, he climbed off of me and lay beside me, smiling as he ran a hand through my hair. "I'm going to remind you that from now on, whenever you come to Safe Haven, you are going to have to wear the collar I gave you and not be able to take it off until you leave. If you lived here, well, then we would have to discuss you wearing it all the time, but you don't have to. I don't want to jeopardize your relationship with Rhys and Braxton. This was why I bought you the anklet as something that you won't take off."

"Thank you, Sir!" I exclaimed and smiled at him. "I know that we will still have a few things to work out once I get to Safe Haven in a couple weeks," I said. I knew that our master/slave relationship was unconventional in that we were not in close proximity, so the rules would not be the same. This meant that the collar he gave me would normally be worn to show others he owned me, but given my thruple with Rhys and Braxton we had other boundaries to consider, but I was all for wearing the collar from the time I got to the hotel to the time I checked out.

Surprised, Dimitri said "You're coming in a couple weeks?"

I started to giggle. "I haven't told the guys yet, but I thought it might be a good time to start our master/slave relationship in full."

"Oh god, love that is going to be awesome. I am looking forward to starting our master/slave relationship and also having dates with you outside of Safe Haven."

"I was thinking about those dates," I said and saw Dimitri beam happily. "Since those dates will be under the guise of master and slave, we should try to have one every 6 weeks max."

"My little slave, you have thought this through, haven't you?"

"Sort of," I replied. "I think a lot will depend upon how often I am coming to Safe Haven."

"Well, I am thinking every couple of weeks. You will need time with Cassidy and Bella too so that they can work more with your dominant side. I highly doubt that you will be allowed to be my slave those weekends."

"Well, couldn't we have our dates then?" I asked.

"Honestly, only if Rhys and Braxton aren't coming. Call me selfish, but I am not working the day we have our date. I plan to enjoy every moment with you I can."

I could feel myself blushing which was something I didn't do often and Dimitri noticed because he started to chuckle and said to me, "Are you blushing?"

"Stop!" I swatted him. "I'm blushing at the thought of you and me on a date and nobody else. I was thinking about how we might end up back here at your house."

"I can be a gentleman for you," he said and I started to laugh and so did he.

"But I don't want you to be a gentleman. I love you just as you are," I said and then kissed him, my arms wrapped around his neck and sat on his lap straddling him. Beneath me, his cock slowly stirred to life. Feeling his cock slowly rise to the occasion was tantalizing and that need for his cock to be buried deep inside my pussy great.

As if he could read my mind, Dimitri slid his cock into my vagina and placed his hands on my hips and slowly started to pound me. Our bodies in sync as he hammered his hardness into me, I couldn't help but come my sweet nectar drowning his erection as I continued to ride him. He satisfied me in every way possible and he knew it based on my moans. I couldn't wait to feel him releasing his seed deep inside me once again.

"Going to come!" he moaned as he shot his hot milky substance deep inside of me once again.

Together we collapsed on the bed all spent from our extracurricular activities, but we were satiated. "We should get a little rest while we can so we don't look like we've been fucking all night," he suggested to me. I could only laugh out loud before I found the right words to say. "So, what if we do look like we've been fucking all night, because it's true."

Shaking his head and smiling he said, "So incorrigible. I can't wait to properly punish you as my slave."

"And you know I am going to love every moment of it Eros." I decided to use Eros instead of Dimitri just to remind him that I knew my place in the relationship, but I would push the boundaries when I could. Dimitri was right though; we should get a little shut eye and truthfully, I was excited to sleep with him.

⌢⌢ Chapter 10

Morning came all too quickly for us it felt like, but I also knew we had others to go back to. I was curious though to see how the night went for Rhys, Braxton, Cassidy, and Bella. If I knew them like I thought I did I was betting that they all had a fabulous night, and like Dimitri had said, probably switched partners at some point or other.

"I'm sad to see the sunrise," Dimitri said with a forlorn look in his face and I could empathize with him.

"I know what you mean, but we're going to figure it out and then be able to act accordingly."

"We should probably head on out since I have to get breakfast heated up and coffee brewing."

"You cooked breakfast?" Shocked, I was shocked and impressed at this man because of the cooking he did. Not only could he cook, but made some of the most delicious food I have had.

"Yeah. In another lifetime I was becoming a chef," he said nonchalantly.

"What? Really?"

"I will tell you about it on our first date. Deal?"

"Damn, that's a long time!" I pouted, "but it will be worth the wait," I said and smiled.

When we walked out of the bedroom it was silent throughout the house. I guess nobody was awake yet, but I also knew that the silence could be deceiving since everyone were masters and mistresses so they could be quiet when they wanted to.

Dimitri grabbed the breakfast casserole and put it in the oven, I was busy getting the coffee brewing. I could've waited for him to finish getting breakfast in the oven but truth was, I really wanted a cup of coffee.

While Dimitri and I sat cuddling on the couch with coffees in hand, everyone was slowly stirring and coming out from the bedrooms.

"Mm is that coffee I smell?" said Cassidy.

"Sure is. Help yourself, but I can't promise it's taste because Mackenzie made the pot," Dimitri said and started laughing as I smacked him with my free hand. Both Rhys and Braxton were chuckling at Dimitri's response as well.

I couldn't help but smile because this was nice – all of it. Everyone appeared to be in a good mood, too bad it was coming to an end. While I couldn't speak for Braxton, I could only assume that he had a wonderful birthday weekend just about as much as I did. I was glad that we decided to come to Safe Haven to celebrate, because it ended up reminding me just how important these friends were. Plus, Dimitri and I were fixing to embark on a few new adventures together and that had me all excited.

 *A few hours later...*

Rhys, Braxton, and I had checked out of the hotel and were in the car on the way back home. Once again, our visit to Safe Haven was titillating but held special meaning for us since we had celebrated mine and Braxton's birthdays with our friends who embraced this alternative lifestyle. Who knew that in less than a year I had overcome my shyness about sex and actually found myself enjoying BDSM and I was discovering that I was a sadomasochist as I quite thoroughly enjoyed the pain that I got and received, especially when I was with Dimitri. Safe Haven had opened up something deep inside of me that I once would have considered taboo, but embraced it and fell in love with those taboo ideas. Hell, I was part of a triad, and now was going to be in a Master/ Slave relationship with Dimitri.

Life for me was changing, and as it changed, I was discovering more about myself than I thought possible. I was enjoying the changes that I was undergoing. I knew that those at Safe Haven were already starting to see the difference in me. I wasn't that shy woman that walked into Safe

Haven after giving her boyfriend her complete trust in him, but was the woman who was open to the alternative lifestyle, and more tolerant of those who chose to live it as well.

Don't miss out!

Visit the website below and you can sign up to receive emails whenever Stephanie Doering publishes a new book. There's no charge and no obligation.

https://books2read.com/r/B-A-AEBUB-NKPIF

BOOKS 2 READ

Connecting independent readers to independent writers.

Also by Stephanie Doering

Safe Haven

Safe Haven

Naughty Indulgences:The Ultimate Birthday Gift

The Weeping Ridge Series

The Ghosts of Willowtree Manor

Standalone

The Weekend Getaway

Claiming Her

Club Abyss

Watch for more at https://books2read.com/author/
stepjhanie-doering/subscribe/1/809276/.